'Dazza and Gregg have linked up well down the right, playing a clever one-two that the coach has shown them in training. Now Dazza swings over a low cross into the middle. Who's there to meet it? It's Brain . . .'

Luke broke out of his commentary mode in alarm. 'Brain!' he gasped. 'What's *he* doing there? I told him to stay out on the wing!'

Brain connected with a classic, right-foot volley, high off the ground. It almost gave the keeper a ricked neck with the speed that the ball flew past him to billow out the netting.

'Fantastic goal!' Gregg whooped. 'A blinder. The school team could do with a few like that.'

Luke wandered back alone to the halfway line, lost in thought. 'Hmm, you're dead right there, Gregg. They could indeed . . .'

FOOTBALL DAFT

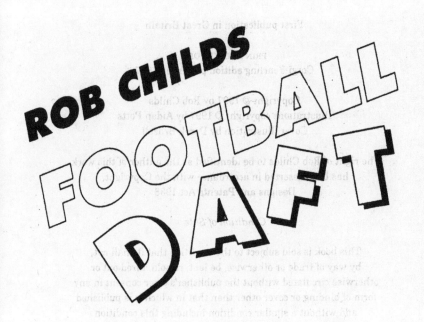

ILLUSTRATED BY
AIDAN POTTS

CORGI YEARLING BOOKS

FOOTBALL DAFT
A CORGI YEARLING BOOK: 0440 863538

First publication in Great Britain

PRINTING HISTORY
Corgi Yearling edition published 1997

Set in 12/15pt Linotype Century Schoolbook by
Phoenix Typesetting, Ilkley, West Yorkshire

Corgi Yearling Books are published by Transworld Publishers Ltd,
61–63 Uxbridge Road, Ealing, London W5 5SA,
in Australia by Transworld Publishers (Australia) Pty. Ltd,
15–25 Helles Avenue, Moorebank, NSW 2170,
and in New Zealand by Transworld Publishers (NZ) Ltd,
3 William Pickering Drive, Albany, Auckland.

The Random House Group Limited supports The Forest Stewardship
Council® (FSC®), the leading international forest-certification organisation.
Our books carrying the FSC label are printed on FSC®-certified paper.
FSC is the only forest-certification scheme supported by the leading
environmental organisations, including Greenpeace. Our
paper procurement policy can be found at
www.randomhouse.co.uk/environment

Printed and bound in Great Britain by Clays Ltd, St Ives plc

Especially for dyslexic readers

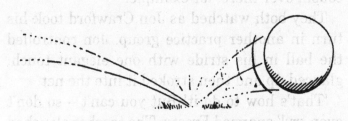

1 Shooting Practice

'No, no, no!' screamed the sports teacher. 'Go and fetch it – run!'

'Frosty' Winter struggled to keep hold of his temper – especially when the boy went and fell over the ball as he tried to dribble it back.

'Look, how many times have I told you, lad?' Frosty ranted. 'It's no good shooting from outside the area like that. You can't even get your shots on target from three metres, never mind thirty!'

Luke Crawford put on his best pained expression. He thought Frosty's criticism was a mite exaggerated. He'd been no more than twenty-five metres out at the most. 'But, you see, sir . . .' he began.

'I haven't got time for any of your rambling excuses,' the teacher cut in. 'Just leave the shooting to people who *can* shoot, OK? Like your cousin over there, for example.'

They both watched as Jon Crawford took his turn in another practice group. Jon controlled the ball in his stride with one elegant touch, glanced up and then stroked it into the net.

'That's how to do it! But you can't – so don't even try!' snapped Frosty. The teacher slouched away to find another hapless victim, leaving Luke to grin somewhat sheepishly at the other players in his group.

'Bit cruel, that,' said Gregg. 'Over the top, I'd say.'

'Yeah, but that's where Luke's effort went, too,' sniggered Gregg's identical twin, Gary. 'Right over the top of the goal!'

'I don't know how you put up with Frosty's sarcasm, Luke,' said Gregg. 'Why do you keep coming when it's obvious he doesn't want you here?'

'Simple. I want to play in the school team.'

'But he never picks you.'

10

'He does sometimes – when he has no other choice!'

'You're football daft, you are, Luke!' laughed Gary. 'I'd have thought being skipper, player-manager and coach of the Swifts would be enough for anybody, but you still want to play for the Comp as well!'

'Somebody has to. And I've got an even better chance now, haven't I?'

That was true. Frosty was facing a rebellion. Three boys had already dropped out of Swillsby Comprehensive's small Year 8 soccer squad, fed up of Frosty's black moods. Now he was in danger of losing his captain.

Matthew Clarke had failed to attend the last two training sessions, giving flimsy excuses, and this time had not bothered to tell the teacher at all. As Frosty fished the practice balls out of the sports store, he overheard the twins gossiping outside.

'Has Matt gone straight home?' asked Gregg.

'Yep,' replied Gary. 'Said he was only going to play Sunday football for the Panthers. Reckoned the Comp's got even worse than the Swifts!'

'Oh, come on, the school team isn't *that* bad yet.'

Gary grinned. 'And we should know – we play for both!'

Frosty was incensed. 'Right, if Clarke's not interested, then neither am I!' he seethed. 'No individual is bigger than the team. We'll just have to do without him.'

Luke's group had their attention refocused on the matter in hand by the demands of their goal-keeper. 'C'mon, you lot!' cried Sanjay. 'Whose go is it? I'm freezing standing here while you're all rabbiting on.'

'I'll warm old Dracula up,' Gregg smiled, using their pet nickname for the eccentric Sanjay Mistry who kept goal for Swillsby Swifts and the

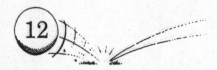

Comp. If his bizarre behaviour between the posts didn't startle the opposition, it certainly scared the life out of his teammates!

Gregg tapped the ball a little way ahead of him and let fly from the edge of the penalty area. The shot had pace but, sadly, not the accuracy Gregg had intended, and Sanjay mocked him unmercifully.

'Looks like you getting warmed up, junior,' Gary chuckled, rubbing in his big brother status, being ten minutes older. 'Go on, chase after it!'

'Why did I have to get lumbered with you dummies?' the goalie moaned in jest. 'I've hardly had a save to make yet.'

'That's only because you've let everything past you,' Gary teased him.

'I couldn't even reach most of 'em!'

Big Ben collected another spare ball to try his luck. 'Reckon Frosty's deliberately put us Swifts together so we don't mess up his other groups,' he remarked. 'He thinks we're all useless.'

'He's right as well,' put in Tubs, the Swifts' overweight full-back.

'You speak for yourself,' Gary replied.

'OK, let's see how wonderful you are.'

'Big Ben's before me. He can show us how it's done.'

13

'Remember I haven't got my specs on,' the defender smiled, but he did at least manage to trouble Sanjay. The goalkeeper had to walk over and bend down to pick up his trickling, mis-hit slice.

'Thanks, Big Ben. Nice to have the ball in my hands again, just to remind me what it feels like.'

'C'mon, then, Gary, your turn,' said Big Ben as the goalkeeper threw the ball back towards the group. 'Smash one in and shut him up.'

Gary worked the ball onto his favoured left foot, took aim and fired, low and hard. But his shot was much too near the keeper and Sanjay merely stuck out his leg to knock it away.

'Couldn't be bothered to dive,' Sanjay laughed. 'Too easy!'

'Right, save this belter, then,' cried Tubs, hoping to fool him with a side-footer instead of thumping the ball in his usual toe-end style.

Sanjay treated his tame trundler with contempt, leaning on the post as the ball bobbled wide. 'Is that the best you people can do?' he snorted. 'You've all had three goes now and nobody's managed to score.'

Luke resolved to set a captain's example. Surrounded by so many Swifts, it felt as though

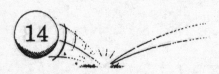

14

he was running his weekly practice with his own Sunday League side. He was determined to score. To make sure, he unwittingly took Frosty's advice and pushed the ball nearer and nearer the goal to give Sanjay no chance.

'Come closer, why don't you?' Sanjay taunted him, standing calmly on his goal-line. 'Are we gonna shake hands before you shoot?'

Luke almost reached the six-yard box before he pulled the trigger – but the gun blew up in his face. Somehow the ball got trapped between his feet and he skewed the shot wildly across the face of the goal. As he sank to his knees in

disbelief, the rest collapsed in hilarity, bringing their shooting practice to an abrupt and sloppy end.

By contrast, Frosty finished the session with an intensive game of two-touch football in the training grids, demanding maximum effort and concentration. Despite the fact that he was a well-qualified, experienced soccer coach, Frosty was never the most tolerant of teachers. Today, after the business over Matthew, he was more grumpy than normal with anybody who made a mistake. Even Jon, their leading scorer, felt the rough edge of his tongue when he attempted only a half-hearted tackle to win the ball.

'Get in the game more, lad!' Frosty yelled at him. 'You're bone-idle sometimes. What's the use of having all those skills on the ball if you don't get it in the first place?'

Luke feared that his cousin was going to respond with one of his casual little shrugs of the shoulders. And when Jon did go and do exactly that, Luke waited for the explosion.

He didn't have to wait long. The volcano blew its top almost instantly and Jon was sent back to the changing rooms. 'Go on!' Frosty roared. 'Off home you go as well and join our dear captain in front of the telly!'

As Jon trailed away, still in a daze about what he'd done wrong, the game continued in near silence. Even the bubbly Luke was subdued, upset by his talented cousin's humiliating treatment. Jon's laid-back style of play might make it appear as if he didn't care, but Luke knew that wasn't the case. Unlike himself, Jon was just too cool to let it show how much he really loved his football.

'Brilliant, Frosty, there goes our best player,' Luke murmured bitterly under his breath. 'Serves you right if I'm the only one left soon – and then you'll have to pick me!'

2 Running Commentary

'Right, men,' cried Luke, poised at the door of the changing hut to lead his team out on to the pitch. 'All ready?'

'Ready, Skipper!' the Swifts called back as usual to humour their captain, avoiding each other's eyes to prevent any outbreak of the giggles.

'Er . . . I'm not, Skipper, hang on a minute,' appealed Sean, Swifts' left-side midfielder. 'I've not finished combing my hair yet.'

There were groans all round. 'What a poser!' cackled Sanjay. 'He must reckon the crowd's here just to admire his hairstyle!'

Tubs glanced out through a hole in the wooden planking. 'Crowd! He calls five and a half people a crowd?'

'Half?' queried Luke, impatiently. 'Titch is in here with us!'

'Oh, no, sorry, it's your dad. He's just stood up!'

'Pity you're not watching, Tubs,' grinned Sanjay. 'You'd swell the size of any crowd!'

'C'mon, will you, Sean!' Luke demanded. 'What's the use, anyway? It's chucking it down out there. We'll all look like drowned rats in a minute.'

'It's not exactly dry in here,' grumbled Titch. 'There's a leak in the roof over me.'

'S.O.S.,' cried Tubs. 'Titch is getting washed away.'

'Need a tidal wave to carry you off,' Titch said, adding to the friendly insults hurling about the ramshackle hut.

Luke sometimes wished his players would approach a vital league match a little more seriously. Especially with the looming prospect of relegation. He tried again to recapture their attention, tapping the logo on the front of his gold shirt. 'OK, team. Let's make this another *GREAT GAME*!'

'For them or for us?' grunted Brain,

their disorganized left-winger.

Luke stared at him. 'You've got odd socks on again!'

Brain gazed down at his mixed pair of gold and red socks. 'Yeah, soz, Skipper. In a bit of a hurry this morning.'

Luke closed his eyes and offered up a quick, silent prayer for mercy. He knew they would certainly need some extra help from somewhere. Despite the state of the home team's changing hut and the ridiculous name they'd given themselves, Real Marwood demanded respect. They were the league's top scorers and pushing hard for promotion.

Real were not in the mood to let either the heavy rain or the feeble opposition distract them from their ambitions. Their manager screamed his nonstop instructions from the touchline, displaying a colourful, if limited, vocabulary. And when Real scored the opening goal, he jumped about as though somebody had put a firework down his trousers.

The Swifts' adult duo, by contrast, showed all the animation of a damp squib, huddled under Luke's uncle's large umbrella. 'Don't know why our lads always look so amazed when they let a

22

goal in,' Uncle Ray commented wryly. 'You'd think they'd be used to it.'

Luke's dad glanced up at his bearded younger brother. 'That's down to Luke, I reckon,' he said. 'He keeps telling them so often how much they're improving that maybe they're beginning to believe him.'

Ray chuckled. 'Doubt it. More likely they're not fully aware just how bad they really are!'

'That's a bit harsh. The main thing is, they're still enjoying their football. Results aren't every-thing, you know.'

'Good job, or the manager and coach might have got the sack by now.'

'Who, us? But we don't do anything. We leave it all to Luke.'

'Exactly!' grinned Ray. 'Just look at him now, charging around as if the future of the world was at stake.'

They gazed at Luke, partly in admiration and partly in pity, as the number nine chased the ball all over the pitch. His hyperactivity was occasionally rewarded with the odd kick, some-times in the wrong direction, but everybody knew if the Swifts' skipper was anywhere near. They would pick up this buzzing sound in their

ears, as irritating as radio interference. It was Luke's habitual running commentary.

'*The Swifts need to hit back quickly after Real's lucky first goal. Inspired by their skipper, who's involved in every move, they launch a dangerous raid down the left wing where Brain has the beating of his marker. Brain shows him the ball then whips it away out of reach, slipping it inside to the skipper in space . . .*'

Sadly, Luke wasn't in as much space as he thought. Carried away by his biased commentary, he didn't know there was a defender trotting along behind him. The ball slid under

his boot to his laughing opponent and with barely a pause, Luke turned and raced off again in pursuit.

'Robbed of possession by a wicked bobble on the bumpy, rain-sodden pitch, the skipper doubles back to get ball-side again, tireless as ever in supporting his players. Wherever they look to find him and help them out of trouble, Luke Crawford is there . . .'

In reality, outside Luke's world of fantasy football, it meant that he was liable to pop up anywhere to get in their way. Not by coincidence, the Swifts' only worthwhile shot of the first half

managed to escape Luke's intervention. Brain's jinking solo run took him skilfully through three challenges, but he saw his low drive well saved by the otherwise unemployed home keeper.

Sanjay was kept somewhat busier. The ball that beat him for the fourth goal skimmed over the wet grass like a flat stone across a lake before its loopy trajectory finally eluded his flailing arms.

'Four—nil!' groaned Dazza, the right-winger, as they all tried to creep under Ray's umbrella at half-time. 'I've hardly touched the ball yet.'

'Lucky you,' said Big Ben. 'Us defenders haven't had a second's rest. Why don't you come back and help out if you're so bored?'

'I'm ready for a breakaway, aren't I? You tell 'em, Skip.'

'That's right,' Luke confirmed. 'We can't give up hope of scoring and getting back into this game, men . . .'

Gary cut in. Luke hadn't succeeded in giving a team talk all season without being interrupted. 'What do you mean, getting *back* into the game? We've never even been in it once yet!'

'Well, it's about time we were, then, isn't it?' Luke replied. 'Let's try and give *them* something to worry about for a change . . .'

'Like whether they're gonna be able to reach double figures or not,' suggested Tubs.

'Rubbish!' Luke scoffed. 'They're not going to score ten against us.'

Luke was right. Real Marwood had rattled up *twelve* goals by the time the referee's whistle piped its last soggy peep and saved the Swifts from further punishment. The second half was a fiasco – from Titch's deflected own goal to Sean's late decision to duck out of the way of a goal-bound screamer.

'Not going to head that one,' Sean said. 'Might have given me a second parting on the wrong side!'

'I'll part your hair again for you,' Sanjay growled, sitting in a muddy puddle. 'With an axe!'

The only silver lining in the Swifts' storm clouds was their single goal. It came as a mere consolation when they were already so far behind that not even the Real manager could bother to utter more than a couple of curses in response to criticize his team's slack marking.

'Dazza and Gregg have linked up well down the right, playing a clever one-two that the coach has shown them in training. Now Dazza swings over a low cross into the middle. Who's there to

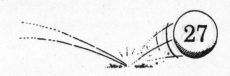

meet it? It's Brain . . .'

Luke broke out of his commentary mode in alarm. 'Brain!' he gasped. 'What's *he* doing there? I told him to stay out on the wing!'

Brain connected with a classic, right-foot volley, high off the ground. It almost gave the keeper a ricked neck with the speed that the ball flew past him to billow out the netting.

'Fantastic goal!' Gregg whooped. 'A blinder. The school team could do with a few like that.'

Luke wandered back alone to the halfway line, lost in thought. 'Hmm, you're dead right there, Gregg. They could indeed . . .'

The Swifts' captain was so preoccupied, he went automatically to the centre-spot and prepared to kick off again.

'Don't you reckon you've done that enough today?' smirked Real's centre-forward, already with four of his side's goals to his credit. 'Let us have a go for a change, eh? I haven't scored from here yet!'

29

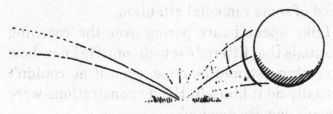

3 Want to Play?

The sports hall of Swillsby Comprehensive echoed to the sounds of pounding feet, shouts and footballs smacking against its walls. It wasn't any of the school teams doing extra training on a dark Wednesday evening, but the Swifts hard at work improving their soccer skills.

At least that was the general idea behind Luke persuading Dad to book the hall for an hour each week during the winter. He'd even had Uncle Ray filming the first few sessions so that the players could study their own techniques on video tape.

Sadly, as with most of Luke's ideas, things tended not to go quite to plan. The players were too busy enjoying a good kick-about to pay much heed to his coaching – and the filming stopped after a stray pass from Dazza hit Ray on the head and made him drop the camcorder. Head, glasses, camera and Dazza's passing were all in need of some remedial attention.

Luke spent hours poring over the coaching manuals that littered his bedroom. He knew how everything should be done, even if he couldn't actually do it himself. His demonstrations were always eagerly awaited.

'Look,' he began, halting a group practising their chipping. 'You have to make sure you get more underneath the ball to lift it . . .'

'Titch is the only one here who could get *underneath* the ball, Skip,' put in Dazza quickly, deliberately trying to sidetrack him.

Luke pressed on regardless. 'If you place your non-kicking foot just there, see, and lean back . . .'

This time it was Gary who interrupted him. 'Where was that again?'

'Just there,' repeated Luke, showing them once more. 'If you place your left foot well behind the ball, then with your right . . .'

'But I kick with my left foot, remember,' Gary persisted. 'I only use the right one for standing on!'

Luke sighed, realizing what they were up to. 'OK, just do everything the opposite way to what I'm saying.'

'Oh, that's easy, then,' Gary grinned. 'I do that anyway!'

'Just watch me,' said Luke, hoping to appear confident. 'This is how to chip a ball to a team-mate over somebody's head.'

He took a few steps back from the ball and

then paused. 'I'll aim to chip it about as high as that basketball ring on the wall, right?'

'Right, Skipper,' they nodded, trying to look serious.

Luke trotted in, picturing in his mind the illustrations from the books that made it seem so simple. Unfortunately he misjudged his run-up and plonked his left foot down too far behind the ball. He had to overstretch to reach it and slipped, toppling backwards as the ball trickled mockingly across the tiled floor.

Luke hauled himself to his feet with as much dignity as he could muster in the circumstances, ignoring the stifled giggles. 'Yes, well, it does take a bit of practice to get it right,' he said, giving a little cough. 'But that's what we're here for, isn't it?'

'That's true, Skipper,' grinned Big Ben. 'Would you . . . er . . . just show us again what you did. I'm not quite certain how to break my fall safely when I try to copy that!'

Luke shot him a dirty look. 'Brain!' he called out. 'Come over here a minute, will you, and show these clodhoppers how to chip a ball properly.'

'Which foot, Skipper?' Brain asked.

34

'Either, doesn't matter.'

'Good, 'cos I'm never sure which is which,' Brain admitted.

'Just wish more of us had two good feet like you,' Luke said in genuine envy.

'Yeah, as long as you don't try and kick with both at the same time,' Dazza cackled.

Brain did what came naturally to him. He'd never read a coaching book in his life. In fact, he'd barely read any book in his life. With his dyslexic difficulties, he struggled to make sense of even the most basic sentences on his bad days.

This was one of his good ones. He chipped the first ball with his slightly stronger left foot, making perfect contact to send the ball slapping high against the far wall. He changed the angle of his approach for the next demonstration, using his other foot. This time the ball curled up and, to everyone's sheer amazement, thudded into the backboard and plopped down through the basketball ring.

'Did you mean to do that?' gasped Gary.

Brain grinned and shook his head. 'Course not. Sliced that one a bit. Bet I couldn't do it again if I stood here and tried all night.'

'OK, see if the rest of you can,' said Luke,

seizing the opportunity to give them some incentive. 'I just want a little word with old Brain here.'

He took the winger to one side of the hall to sit on a bench. 'I've been thinking . . .' Luke began.

'Oh, oh! I'm not sure I'm gonna like the sound of this,' said Brain.

'No, listen, would you like to play a bit more football each week?'

'How can I when the Swifts play every Sunday?'

'I mean for the school,' said Luke. 'Why don't you come and play for the Comp as well? We need someone like you.'

'*We?*' he queried. 'I didn't know you played in the school team.'

'Well, not every game,' Luke smiled, bending the truth to suit his own purpose. 'But we're not doing very well this season, and having you on the wing would be great. Might make all the difference.'

Brain shook his head. 'Soz, Skipper. I'm not gonna suffer all Frosty's snide comments again. I went to a few practices in the first year and he used to get at me something rotten.'

'Yes, but you're loads better now. Look how well you've been playing for the Swifts.'

Brain stood up and started to walk away. 'Ta for the offer,' he said, turning back for a moment. 'I like playing for the Swifts and I don't want Frosty to go and spoil things. I nearly gave up soccer altogether 'cos of him.'

'Well, I did try,' Luke sighed as Brain rejoined his group. 'Perhaps I'll have another go at him after he's thought it over for a few days.'

Luke organized the players into a six-a-side game of two-touch football – a very optimistic ruling when most of them usually needed half a dozen attempts to control a ball. They did their best, however, playing with an enthusiasm that would do credit to a team at the top of the league. Their 12–1 defeat was never mentioned. It was taken for granted; they were half-expecting another thrashing next Sunday as well from whoever they were up against.

After Luke blazed a shot over Sanjay's low crossbar, Uncle Ray managed to catch his attention. 'Somebody to see you,' he growled, hoicking a thumb in the direction of the door.

'Frosty!' Luke gulped. 'What's he doing here?'

'No idea, but I'm not speaking to that chap at the moment. Jon came home today and told me Frosty's gone and dropped him for Saturday's match. The man must be an idiot.'

'He is,' nodded Luke. 'Jon's not exactly flavour of the month with him right now after what happened last week.'

'Aye, I know. Thought it'd all blow over, but it seems Frosty wants to make a point. Get rid of him quick, will you, before I say something I might regret.'

Luke strolled across to the teacher. 'Hello, sir, come to spy on us, have you, and pick up a few tips?'

'You must be joking!' rasped Frosty. 'I'm surprised to see you lot here. Just popped back to pick up something I'd left behind and I couldn't believe my eyes.'

'Why's that, sir?'

'You mean the Swifts actually practise?' Frosty said, and Luke could tell he was building up to one of his so-called witticisms. 'Amazing! Didn't know you had to practise so hard at being so bad!'

Luke decided to remain silent, tempted though he was to point out that the school team's results this season had been little better. After all, he should know. Luke was obsessed with keeping soccer statistics. He recorded full details in his little black notebooks, not only of every Swifts' match, but of the school team's too.

39

'Anyway,' Frosty said, changing the subject and looking a shade embarrassed. 'I was going to ask you tomorrow, but seeing as you're here now, well . . .'

Luke waited patiently, enjoying the teacher's obvious discomfort. 'It's just that we are . . . um . . . a bit short-staffed, like,' Frosty stumbled on, 'and I was wondering if you were doing anything on Saturday morning . . .'

Frosty trailed away, leaving Luke to draw his own conclusions. 'You mean, you want me to be a sub in the league match against St Paul's?'

Frosty shuffled his feet and gave a sort of sheepish leer. 'Actually, I was thinking about playing you right from the start. Reckon you deserve the chance in a way, attending every practice like you do.'

Luke drew in a sharp breath. This was music to his ears. He'd only ever been included in the Comp's starting line-up once before – and he preferred to draw a veil over that personal disaster.

He swallowed hard before trusting his voice to reply. 'Yes, I think I'll be free to play that day, sir!' he said simply.

What he really wanted to do was to jump up

40

and down, clench his fists in delight and run about the hall, shouting at the top of his voice, 'I'm in! I'm in! I've finally made it!'

That would have to wait until he was by himself later . . .

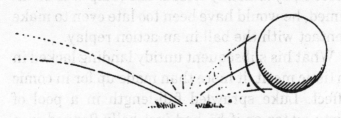

4 From Bad to Worse

'*And now here's Luke Crawford, the Comp's new striker, promoted into the First Team in their hour of need. He's ghosted deep into the Saints' penalty area and nobody's picked him up. If only Swillsby can get the ball to him. The deadly number nine just doesn't miss chances like this . . .*'

Luke not only did miss the chance when it came, he totally missed the ball as well. Gary had spotted Luke lurking by the far post, unmarked, and swung over a long cross towards him. The full-back merely hoped for the best – but feared the worst. And so it proved.

Luke had been left unmarked for two reasons. Firstly, because St Paul's were already 5–0 up and rapidly losing interest in the contest – and secondly, because their defenders had already written off the number nine as posing no threat. The ball sailed over their heads and Luke rose to meet it, eyes firmly closed. His jump was so ill-timed, he would have been too late even to make contact with the ball in an action replay.

What his subsequent untidy landing lacked in artistic merit, it more than made up for in comic effect. Luke sprawled full-length in a pool of dirty water as if he had just belly-flopped in a race at a swimming gala.

He picked himself up out of the mire, his black and white striped shirt now looking more like it belonged to an All Blacks rugby team.

'Penalty!' Luke appealed. 'Somebody pushed me as I jumped.'

'There was nobody near you, lad,' Frosty growled back, wishing he could blow the whistle instead for full time. The weakened Comp side had been completely outplayed by the visitors, and the teacher could just imagine the gleeful reaction of Matthew and co. when they heard the result. The very thought of it made his teeth ache!

Matthew had been openly forecasting an annihilation all week. 'Without me and you, Adam, the Comp's gonna get murdered!' he chortled to his Padley Panthers' teammate.

'And Jon,' Adam reminded him. 'Frosty's gone and lost all three of his Panthers' stars now.'

'Yeah, careless of him,' Matthew grinned. 'He'll have to come begging on his hands and knees before I might consider playing for the Comp again!'

'Me too,' said Adam, looking at the team sheet on the sports noticeboard. 'He must be desperate. Half of this lot are Swifts!'

Matthew could not contain his mirth. 'Well, if there's one thing Loony Luke's Sloths are good at, it's getting thrashed!'

Sanjay and the Garner twins were the only Swifts to be regulars for the school too. Even that, Gary believed, was because Frosty couldn't tell him and Gregg apart so didn't know which one to drop. Now they had been joined by Luke, Big Ben and Tubs to make up the numbers. The Swifts almost felt at home as the score mounted up against them.

'Still time to get a goal or two back ourselves, Gregg,' Luke insisted as the sixth flashed past Sanjay. 'Never give up.'

Gregg shook his head in admiration. 'Somehow you always look on the bright side of any disaster. You'd make the sinking of the *Titanic* sound like a good chance to practise lifeboat drill!'

Luke was simply relieved that, for once, he had not been the cause of the crushing defeat. He had after all only given one penalty away so far.

'*Just a few minutes left of a one-sided match, but Luke Crawford refuses to give up hope,*' droned his commentary. '*He wins the ball back in midfield, but his pass catches Tubs sleeping*

and a Saints striker is through on goal. Sanjay comes out to narrow the angle – oh, dear! Seven–nil.'

That was it. Frosty could stand no more. He blew the whistle early and stomped off in disgust back to the school building. They had another match coming up the following week – in the cup – and he had no idea what kind of a team he was going to be able to put out.

The prospect of reinstating Matthew stuck in his craw. Jon Crawford, though, was another matter, and Frosty suspected he had perhaps

acted rather too hastily there. He might well have to swallow his pride . . .

As the players trailed in after him, Luke caught sight of a spectator standing over by the hedge. 'Hi, Brain, how long have you been watching?'

Brain shrugged. 'Dunno, I missed the start.'

'Pity you weren't on the pitch,' Luke said. 'Why don't you change your mind and give it a go next week? I'm sure Frosty would jump at you.'

'Probably jump *on* me,' Brain replied. 'He always used to.'

'C'mon, he's not that bad,' Luke began to argue, but stopped as Brain pulled a face. 'Well, maybe he is, I admit, but things have changed. Right now, old Frosty needs every extra player he can get.'

'I'll think about it.'

'Good man, and don't forget – tomorrow morning, quarter past ten at the changing cabin. Swifts versus the Wanderers.'

'Yeah, don't worry, I'll be there.'

At kick-off time next day, the Swifts were a player short. Their one and only sub had cried off and Brain had still not reported for duty.

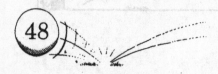

'Where's he got to?' Luke fumed as Uncle Ray went to fetch him. 'Bet he's still trying to find his shorts or something. Typical!'

'He can't help it, you know, Skipper,' Titch said. 'He's just like that, always losing and forgetting things, getting himself muddled up.'

'I know,' Luke sighed. 'But we actually had a chance of a result here against the Wanderers. They're in relegation trouble as well.'

After a heavy overnight frost, the referee had inspected the pitch very carefully before allowing the match to go ahead. 'Best to wear all-weather trainers with extra grip, if you've got them,' he advised the players as they changed in the cabin. 'Anybody in studded boots is going to find it difficult to turn without slipping over.'

'Play the way you're facing,' Luke told his team. 'Keep it simple. Don't try anything too fancy on this surface.'

'No danger of that from us,' said Tubs, giving his distinctive, rumbling laugh. 'These conditions ought to suit us. Bring the other lot down to our level!'

Luke didn't like to agree openly, but privately thought the same. That is, until Brain failed to appear. He was such a key player for the Swifts and the source of most of their goals. The

49

realization that his teammates valued his abilities had done wonders for Brain's own confidence, too, and he had begun to believe in himself far more at last.

Before the game started, Sanjay jumped up to touch the crossbar as usual. It was meant to bring him luck, but any observer studying the Swifts' goals-against column in the league table might have been excused thinking otherwise. 'Glad I'm wearing my trackie bottoms today,' he murmured, stamping on the bone-hard, rutted goalmouth. 'Have to watch the bounce, though.

The ball's sure gonna do some crazy things on this.'

It was the state of the ground, in fact, that enabled Luke to put the ball into the net after just five minutes. Unfortunately, it was his own.

The ball ricocheted to the captain in a crowded Swifts' goalmouth but sat up awkwardly on one of the ruts as Luke attempted a mighty clearance. His wild swing resulted in the most horrendous slice off the outside of his trainer that sent the ball spiralling back over Sanjay's head. If Dracula's looks could kill, the team would have needed a new skipper!

Two minutes later, this time at the right end, Luke seemed to have made amends for his gross error. Dazza crossed the ball low into the Wanderers' area and a cruel bounce fooled everyone – until Luke stuck out a foot.

'Goooaaalll!!! The skipper has equalized!' blared out the ecstatic commentary as the scorer danced about the penalty area.

Even in his frenzy, the small part of Luke's mind that remained in gear began to wonder why none of his teammates were racing to join in his celebrations. They had all heard something that had failed to register on Luke's consciousness – the referee's whistle.

'Sorry, lad, no goal,' the official said, trying to calm him down. 'You were offside when the ball was passed.'

The bad news had the desired effect. Even Luke's commentary held a minute's silence to mark his grief – and this was extended further when the Wanderers went and increased their lead. Big Ben's centre-back partner, Mark, fell over at the wrong moment, allowing an attacker a clear sight of goal. Sanjay's lucky charm once again failed to work any magic.

It was at that moment that Brain finally made his appearance, scrambling out of Ray's car. 'Soz, guys,' he apologized. 'Must have misread my watch. Didn't realize what the time was.'

'Haven't you got any trainers?' whined Luke.

'Yeah, but I couldn't find them. Think I must have left them behind in the sports hall after our practice. Won't my boots be all right?'

Brain got his answer the first time the ball came out to him on the left wing. He tried a dummy shuffle to bamboozle his opponent and finished up on his backside as his feet slithered from underneath him.

Luke tried hard to keep any note of desperation out of his commentary.

'Can the Swifts just hold out till the interval to give their player-manager time to make some vital changes? Now at full strength at last, they might still stand a chance of winning this match – if only they can actually stand up!'

5 Swap!

'It's stupid playing on a frozen pitch like this,' Sean muttered at half-time. 'Somebody's going to end up with a broken leg.'

'Is that why I haven't seen you make a tackle yet?' Luke asked pointedly. 'It's been like playing with nine men, not ten.'

Sean affected a shrug. 'Well, I've got a date this afternoon and I don't want to have to turn up to it in a wheelchair.'

'A date!' snorted Tubs. 'He's only gonna hang around with a gang of kids outside the village hall, trying to look cool. I've seen 'em there.'

Sean had to suffer a chorus of jeers before Luke managed to focus minds back on the game. 'Look, Brain's side of the pitch second half isn't as bad as the other. Let's make the most of him now he's here and give him the ball as much as possible.'

Brain shook his head sadly. 'Don't rely on me, Skipper. I can't keep my feet in these boots.'

'You'll be OK,' Luke reassured him. 'You'll be wearing trainers.'

'I haven't got any, I told you.'

'You have now,' said Luke, yanking off his own shoes. 'Mine! C'mon, we both take the same size. Give me your boots and we'll do a swap.'

It was the ultimate sacrifice for the captain to make for the good of the team. Luke acknowledged that his own performance might suffer – though perhaps not to a degree that anyone else would notice – but Brain had the special ability that could well swing the match in their favour.

The Swifts responded to Luke's unselfish gesture and started the second half like a team possessed. They threw themselves into tackles to win the ball at all costs and supplied Brain with it at every opportunity.

Even Sean risked life and limb in support of Brain up and down the left flank. After ten minutes' play, he challenged strongly to win a fifty-fifty ball and then tried to exchange a quick one-two pass with Brain to get past a defender. The full-back refused to let them by, deliberately tripping Sean as he ran forward for Brain's return ball.

'Free-kick,' indicated the referee. 'Direct.'

That was all Luke wanted to hear. Standing over the ball to conduct operations, the captain displayed four fingers of his right hand behind his back to the waiting Brain. It was part of a secret signalling code Luke had worked out for use at dead-ball kicks like this, designed to keep the opposition guessing about their intentions.

It confused Brain too. He saw the sign but couldn't remember what it was supposed to mean. He never bothered to revise the code printed in Luke's dossier of tactics given out to every player in the squad. It was all too detailed for him.

As Luke suddenly darted to one side, losing his footing in the process, Brain gave a little shrug and ran in. He struck the ball fiercely, bang on target. It ripped clean through a hole in the defensive wall and powered into the net with the goalkeeper left gaping.

Luke sat on the frosty ground, muttering to himself, 'Four fingers, Brain, four fingers. That means try a curler round the wall, not blast the ball straight through it. Why don't you ever follow instructions?'

Any comeback hopes were almost halted in their tracks a minute later when a header crashed against the Swifts' crossbar. The ball bounced down and out again for Big Ben to clear.

'Over the line, ref!' appealed the Wanderers' captain. 'The ball crossed the line.'

'Not all of it,' ruled the referee, perfectly positioned to make his judgement. 'Sorry, no goal!'

'Phew!' breathed Titch. 'That makes up for your goal which didn't count, Skipper.'

'No, it doesn't,' Luke stated flatly. 'Nothing makes up for that!'

The Swifts had to survive a crucial period of heavy bombardment from the Wanderers. They were rescued once by a brave stop from Sanjay, risking his teeth in a dive among a mass of flying feet, and then by Tubs blocking a shot on the goal-line.

Sanjay grinned as he slapped Tubs on his broad back. 'No way past you, eh, pal? As good as boarding up my goal with wood!'

'Yeah, when Tubs stands in front of the sun, we get a total eclipse!' chortled Gary. 'No offence, of course, Tubs.'

'Good job or I'd knock the living daylights out of both of you,' Tubs responded, letting his laugh rumble on.

It was very much against the run of play, therefore, when the Swifts broke away to snatch the all-important equalizer.

'Sean brings the ball over the halfway line, moving into the space created by Luke Crawford's clever decoy run . . . Oops! The skipper's slipped, but Sean slides a killer pass

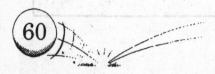

inside the full-back to Brain for the winger to shoot. Oohh! The goalie's saved it, but can't hold on to the ball. It runs loose to Dazza – Goooaaalll!!! Dazza has lashed the rebound high into the net. And now I hand you over to our summarizer . . .'

Luke was also the summarizer, but let his imaginary audience wait for further pearls of wisdom. He didn't want to miss out on the celebrations as Dazza's brilliant white smile lit up Swillsby recreation ground. The Swifts were back on level terms.

Neither team was good enough to conjure up any further goals before the final whistle, both being content in the end to avoid another defeat.

'Told you we could do it, men,' boasted Luke in the cabin afterwards. 'You've just got to have more faith in yourselves – and me!'

'Thanks for the loan of the trainers, Skipper,' said Brain, swapping them again for his boots. 'Er, I've been thinking . . .'

'That makes a nice change,' Luke quipped. 'Did you enjoy it?'

Brain giggled. 'You know what I mean.'

'About giving the school another go?'

Brain nodded. 'Might as well. Seeing as how

the Comp are struggling to raise a team. Didn't want to get shown up there, that's all.'

'No danger of that,' Luke confirmed. 'And no need to worry about Frosty either. You've shown how to cope with one kind of frostbite today, so now you can do it again!'

At home that evening Luke pondered over the successes of the day with quiet satisfaction. Sitting at the desk in his bedroom, he brought his notebook up to date, logging team details, ground conditions and scorers, all in red ink in his neat, small handwriting. It was a task he always looked forward to, even when the Swifts lost heavily, but it wasn't as much fun as composing the match report.

He began to draft out the report that would appear in the next issue of the *Swillsby Chronicle*, the village free newspaper edited by Uncle Ray. He let his nephew loose on the sports page every month to satisfy Luke's growing journalistic ambitions – even though Luke, of course, saw himself becoming a football reporter and television commentator only after his own professional playing career was over. In traditional tabloid style, Luke rarely let the facts get in the way of a good story.

Swifts 2 Wanderers 2

Swillsby Swifts earned another precious
point with a spirited draw against fellow
relegation strugglers, the Wanderers. On a
treacherous, frosty pitch the battling
Swifts – a man short – unluckily trailed 0–2
at half-time. Inspired by their player-manager, Luke Crawford, they fought back with
goals from wingers Brian 'Brain' Draper
and David 'Dazza' Richards. Luke was
robbed of an early strike by a controversial
offside decision, but shrugged off that disappointment and lent leading scorer Brain
his magic goal-grabbing trainers. Brain
repaid the unselfish skipper with a goal
from a well-rehearsed free-kick routine,
cunningly devised by the coach, and then
made the later equalizer for Dazza. 'A fine
team display,' said the modest skipper
afterwards. 'It shows how much the Swifts
have improved this season and we
deserve to avoid the dreaded drop.'

Luke chewed the end of his pen thoughtfully for a minute before putting it down. 'Hmm, that should just about do it,' he murmured, tastefully omitting any mention of his own goal. 'But maybe an extra quote from the coach might be useful to include for the *Chronicle* piece . . .'

His mind wandered on to the school's forthcoming cup game. 'Huh! I find the Comp a new star player, and I bet Frosty won't even thank me for it,' he grunted. 'Just my luck as well if he goes and gives Brain my place in the team!'

Luke chewed the end of his pen thoughtfully for a minute before putting it down. 'Hmm, that should just about do it,' he murmured, tastefully omitting any mention of his own goal. 'But maybe an extra quote from the coach might be useful to include for the Chronicle piece.'

His mind wandered on to the school's forthcoming cup game. 'Huh! I bet the Comp's new star player, and I bet Frosty won't even thank me for it,' he grunted. 'Just my luck as well if he goes and gives Brain my place in the team.'

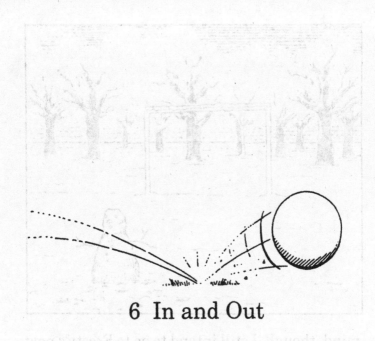

6 In and Out

It snowed the next day. And the next. And the day after that. The rumpled white duvet of snow covering the pitches put an untimely stop to any outdoor practices and the weekend fixtures also had to be cancelled.

Luke's face was as gloomy as the weather. 'Just when things were looking up as well,' he grumbled during a breather at the Swifts' midweek session in the sports hall. 'I reckon we were starting to hit our best form and I'd even managed to get picked for the Comp.'

'Pity!' Brain sympathized. 'I won't change my

mind, though. I still intend to go to Frosty's next practice.'

'Wonder if he'll have sorted things out with the rebels by then?' Gregg chipped in.

'Don't include my cousin with that lot. He was just an innocent victim of Frosty's bad temper,' Luke said. 'Anyway, it's all blown over now. Jon told me yesterday that Frosty has actually apologized for dropping him.'

'Never!' exclaimed Gregg.

Luke nodded. 'Straight up. Wish I'd been there. If I'd caught it on video, I could have made a fortune renting out the tape!'

'Maybe Ray threatened not to let his son play for the school again?'

Luke shrugged. 'It's just great that Jon's back. All star players have ups and downs in their careers, even the legendary Johan Cruyff!'

'The old Flying Dutchman is a real hero of yours, isn't he?' Brain grinned as Gregg chased off after a stray ball.

'Sure is. If I didn't already call my cousin Johan, I might even say you're a bit like the Maestro.'

'You're joking!'

'No, I'm not. The way you can shoot and cross a ball with either foot and dribble like a wizard, it's magic!'

'Thanks, makes a change to get a bit of praise,' said Brain. 'Matt was giving me a hard time again today, trying to show me up as usual.'

'Why was that?'

'Oh, you know Jenkins who takes us for maths? Well, he's been having a blitz on our tables recently and I still can't say them. I just get all muddled up and forget where I am.'

'What's that got to do with Matt?' asked Luke crossly. 'He's not exactly Einstein either when it comes to numbers!'

'Better than me, anyway. He kept coming out

with loud remarks about me being thick and stupid.'

'Didn't Jenkins stop him?'

'Pretended not to hear. I think he's a bit scared of Matt – always lets him get away with things, but not me.' Brain sighed and then added, 'Funny, they reckon he was a bit dyslexic, too, you know.'

'Who, Jenkins?'

'No, Einstein – and he was a genius!'

'Well, at least Miss Elliot in English knows you're not stupid. She often says what good ideas you come out with in discussions and that.'

'Yeah, but I can't get them down on paper, that's the trouble. Can't even spell my own name right sometimes. I don't realize I've got the letters the wrong way round until somebody like Matt makes fun of it.'

'Matt just likes picking on people,' Luke sighed. 'Does it to me as well 'cos he thinks I'm useless at football.'

Brain deliberately didn't say anything, even though Luke paused for a moment, hoping the winger might at least deny Matthew's judgement.

'Anyway,' Luke continued, 'I think Matt's bitten off more than he can chew if he's trying to

get the better of Frosty. Can't see Frosty backing down again. Guess he'll have to pick a new school team captain.'

Brain noticed a little gleam in Luke's eye. 'Don't go raising your hopes,' he said gently.

The melting snow was still lying on the ground in slushy patches when Frosty called an emergency practice session on the Tuesday of the following week. Only fourteen boys were present, including one new face – Brain.

'Pleased to see you here, Brian,' the teacher greeted him, using his proper name, as the boys wandered up to the pitch.

'You can call me Brain, if you like, sir. Most people do.'

'I prefer Brian,' said Frosty gruffly, but then made an effort to appear friendly. 'Heard you've been having a good season with the Swifts. Leading scorer, I gather. You ought to have come and joined us earlier.'

Brain realized that Luke must have been preparing the way in advance for his sudden appearance. 'Thought you had enough players,' he answered, 'but Luke said I might stand a fair chance of getting a game.'

'Well, Luke might be right for once. I'll

see what you can do first.'

Their opponents wanted to rearrange the cup game for Thursday afternoon but Frosty needed to check how many boys were available – and willing – to play. It would mean leaving school early that day.

'Thanks for attending at short notice,' Frosty said to the shivering group around him.

'Anything to have the chance of skipping off school early on Thursday,' laughed Gary. 'I'd be missing maths!'

Frosty actually smiled. 'Before we start the practice, I want you all to meet your new captain. The name's Crawford . . .'

For the briefest of moments, Luke's heart leapt into his mouth, but he did wonder later whether Frosty had done it on purpose – just to tease him.

'Jon Crawford!' Frosty announced after a theatrical pause and Jon grinned bashfully. 'Even if Matthew Clarke ever comes back into the squad, Jon's going to remain captain of the Comp team from now on.'

'Congrats, Johan,' Luke said as the players broke away to warm up. 'You should have been skipper in the first place. Matt was always too

quick to moan at anybody who made a mistake – especially me!'

'Don't worry, Luke,' Jon smiled. 'I won't be getting at you. Just play the best you can, that'll do me.'

Luke hugged himself with delight. With Jon as team captain, he looked forward with fresh optimism to a more regular place in the side, despite the extra competition from Brain. Inevitably, it was the new attacker who caught the eye – Frosty's eye.

The sports teacher didn't have Brain for Games and he was impressed – very impressed

indeed – with what he now saw. 'Can't believe how much this kid has come on since last year,' he muttered to himself.

Frosty was tempted to include Brain immediately in the cup team and his mind was made up in one flash of brilliance. The winger received the ball tight on the left touchline in the seven-a-side game, hemmed in by two players, but slipped through them with a touch of Houdini-like escapology. His quicksilver feet also tricked him past another tackle before he drew Sanjay out of goal and flicked it expertly over the keeper into the net.

Luke looked on like a proud father, assuming full credit for grooming such rare talent. 'Who needs Matthew Clarke now we've got Brain?'

Luke's question was similar to the one that smugly crossed Frosty's mind, doubling up with a feeling of relief. 'With Jon in attack again, along with Brian, I don't have to suffer you-know-who messing things up any more,' Frosty chuckled. 'He'll understand – he's used to it!'

Back in the changing room, Luke found himself nursing the number thirteen shirt, trying to come to terms with the irony of the situation.

'Bad luck!' Jon consoled him. 'Like old friends, you and that shirt!'

Luke nodded sadly. 'Yeah, but I thought it was about time that even the best of pals must part. Didn't want to see it again just yet.'

'Cheer up. I'll put in a good word for you with Frosty and maybe he'll bring you on at half-time on Thursday, OK?'

'Thanks, Johan,' Luke sighed. 'As long as we win, that's the main thing, I guess. Football's a team game, and a manager has to do what he thinks is right for the side.'

'It's tough at the top, eh, Luke? You know all about running a team.'

Luke forced a grin. 'Yeah,' he agreed under his breath. 'But at least on Sundays the manager makes sure his own name is the first one that goes down on the team sheet!'

'No, you can't be excused from my lesson tomorrow,' Mr Jenkins stated firmly. 'Your work is careless and untidy and you're falling behind.'

'B . . . but I'll have to miss the match if I don't get permission to leave early, sir,' Brain said, almost whimpering.

'Tough!' snapped the teacher. 'Better to miss the match, than miss maths. If I thought you'd really been trying and working hard, I might have let you go – just this once.'

'But I *have* been trying, sir,' Brain pleaded. 'It's just that . . .'

'Sorry, Brian, I've made my decision and that's final. You'll just have to inform Mr Winter that you can't play.'

Brain picked up his bag and shuffled out of the classroom, passing a smirking Matthew on the way. 'Thicko!' came the hissing taunt. 'You can't play, anyway. You're rubbish!'

Brain felt his fists clench, but fought down the urge to lash out at his tormentor. Tears prickled behind his eyes, and no way did he want Matthew to see how upset he was.

Gary had to quicken his step to catch up with Brain along the corridor. 'I heard what Jenkins said. What a—'

'Doesn't matter!' Brain cut him off. 'It's my own rotten fault getting involved again. I should have known something like this would happen.'

'It *does* matter,' Gary insisted. 'Jenkins has got no right to stop you from playing for the Comp. We need you. We've got no chance without you.'

Brain glanced at his friend. 'You mean that?'

'Course I do. I wouldn't have said it otherwise. Don't listen to Matt. He's just narked and taking it out on you.'

'What's *he* got to be narked about?'

'Us leaving early tomorrow and missing maths.'

'Doesn't look like I will be now.'

'We'll see about that. C'mon, let's go and find Frosty. The sooner he knows his new star player has been banned, the better!'

'Are you coming with me?'

'You bet. I want to make sure Frosty's gonna do something about it!'

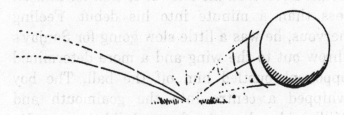

7 Debut Drama

'How did you wangle it with Mr Jenkins, sir?' asked Gary.

The footballers had clambered noisily into the school minibus for Frosty to drive them into town to play against Millbank Comprehensive.

'Easy, Gregg!' Frosty grinned wickedly.

'I'm Gary, sir. Gregg's the ugly one!'

'Ah, yes, Gary, right,' Frosty said, peering round at the twin without showing any real sign of proper recognition. 'I promised him that Brian would stay in two lunchtimes next week to catch up on the work.'

'Oh, thanks very much, sir,' grunted Brain. 'Just what I wanted.'

'Knew you wouldn't mind. Worth the sacrifice, eh?'

'I hope so. Are Millbank any good?'

Brain discovered the answer to that for himself less than a minute into his debut. Feeling nervous, he was a little slow going for Sanjay's throw out to the wing and a more determined opponent bustled him off the ball. The boy whipped a centre into the goalmouth and Millbank's tall centre-forward did the rest. He met the ball with his forehead at point-blank range and sent it hurtling into the net off the underside of the crossbar.

'Show him your fangs next time, Dracula, and he won't dare get that near you again,' muttered Tubs, booting the ball back upfield.

For once, Sanjay didn't respond to the jibe. He was still glaring out at the cowering Brain. Off the pitch, Frosty thought he was watching the start of a horror movie, fearful of the terrors that might lie ahead for his makeshift side.

'C'mon, wake up!' he bellowed at them. 'Get yourselves sorted out. If we wanted to give them a walkover, we needn't have bothered turning up.'

Swillsby were as rattled as their woodwork,

80

but it wasn't Frosty's rantings that finally stung them into action. Luke's touchline commentary captured the vital factor: *'Finding it a struggle without their underrated marksman, Luke Crawford, the Comp look to their new captain, cousin Jon, to steady the sinking ship. Jon controls a pass effortlessly and drifts into Millbank territory like a piece of flotsam after the early wreckage of his side's cup hopes . . .'*

Luke paused for a moment, absurdly pleased with that particular simile, but then a sudden doubt crossed his fertile mind. Was it flotsam or jetsam? He made a mental note to check the

definitions in his dictionary when he got back home. Momentarily distracted, he suddenly realized that Jon was now almost into the Millbank penalty area.

Racing along the side of the pitch, Luke picked up the theme of his commentary where he had left off: '. . . *Is the captain now going to torpedo Millbank's dreams of victory? Jon weaves his silky way past two mesmerized defenders and shoots! Sorry, no he doesn't, but he's fooled the goalie too. The boy dived, but Jon's still got the ball and now just walks it into the empty net. Pure Johan Cruyff!*'

The equalizer stunned Millbank and allowed Swillsby to enjoy the upper hand for the rest of the half. They couldn't score again, but many of their most promising moves came from Brain's skilful runs down the left wing. As his confidence increased, so did his influence on the game, and he created several chances that were squandered by his teammates.

Luke pulled off his tracksuit top during Frosty's team talk, dropping a heavy hint that he expected to be sent on for the second half. 'Keep this up, lads,' Frosty urged them. 'The goals will come.'

'Any subs yet, sir?' asked the captain pointedly.

'No need to make any changes, Jon,' Frosty insisted. 'Like the saying goes, "If it ain't broke, don't fix it!"'

Luke rezipped his top in disappointment and then saw his chances of an appearance lessen when Millbank began the second period like they had the first. Millbank's blue shirts laid siege to Sanjay's goal and the keeper took a knock on the knee as he made a desperate dive at an attacker's feet. While he was still hobbling, he conceded a second goal when the same boy burst past Big Ben to shoot high into the corner.

'Tighter, Ben, get inside his shirt!' yelled Frosty. 'Don't give him space to turn and run at you.'

Once more Swillsby weathered the storm. Their defending wasn't pretty to watch but proved effective enough, with Sanjay on top form. He produced two excellent saves to keep his team in the game, but their own attack was making little headway. Brain was being marked more tightly and not even Jon could repeat his salvage act.

The captain's dribbling forays often ended in cul-de-sacs of defenders, but one of these lone

raids finally earned a free-kick when he was obstructed two metres outside the Millbank penalty area.

'Luke has all kinds of codes in this situation,' Brain grinned, 'but I can't remember any of 'em!'

'No matter.' Jon smiled back. 'My system is more simple. I pass and you shoot, OK?'

'Got it!'

On the referee's whistle, the captain rolled the ball to one side and Brain hit it with his left foot. The ball rose no more than a metre from the ground as it sped towards the goal, taking a slight deflection on the way off somebody's leg to zip past the unsighted keeper.

It was a wonderful moment for Brain. It was worth staying in every lunchtime for the thrill of scoring a goal on his school team debut and being mobbed by his delighted teammates.

Tubs lifted Brain clean off his feet in a great bear hug of congratulations. 'The equalizer! You've done it, Brain!'

'Yeah, you've really gone and done it!' added Gary, and Brain picked up the warning note in his voice.

'What do you mean?'

'Frosty will be looking for some mug to write up a match report for the school magazine.

85

It might be you now.'

Brain felt something squirm in the pit of his stomach, completely erasing all his excitement and pleasure. He could hardly dare trust his voice. 'I didn't know anything about this,' he squeaked.

'Don't you ever read the monthly mag?' Gary asked, and then realized that was a silly question. He saw that his friend's face, recently flushed with blood, had now drained to a ghostly white. 'Sorry, I shouldn't have said anything.'

'Too late,' the winger wheezed. 'Wish I'd gone to maths now!'

'*And there goes the final whistle,*' sighed the commentator wistfully a few minutes after Brain's goal. '*Two apiece, meaning a replay back at Swillsby, but it was hardly a classic cup tie. The unadventurous Swillsby manager, Frosty Winter, made no use of his subs. Bringing on someone like Luke Crawford might well have proven a match-winning gamble . . .*'

Luke was pleased about his protégé's successful debut, but didn't feel like joining in the boisterous celebrations back on board the bus. Brain, too, was strangely subdued, sitting quietly at the end of one of the long seats and

staring out of the gap he'd created in the steamed-up windows.

Luke leant forward and tapped him on the shoulder. 'Thought you'd have been jumping about after a performance like that. Frosty will pick you for every match now. Told you it'd all work out well, didn't I?'

Brain didn't answer, returning his attention to the darkening view outside. Luke caught Gary's eye instead. 'What's the matter? Has somebody said something to upset him?'

'Frosty!' Gary hissed. 'He's asked Brain to

write the match report for the mag to boast how well the team played.'

'I've always wanted to do that!' Luke grumbled. 'Brain's first game and he gets the job straightaway, lucky thing!'

'Don't be daft, Luke – think!' Gary snapped.

'Ah, right,' he murmured when the penny dropped. 'I see – sorry.'

He realized also why Brain felt unable to refuse. Frosty would be the last person to understand anything about his dyslexic difficulties. Luke poked Brain in the back. 'Don't worry,' he whispered. 'I'll help you . . .'

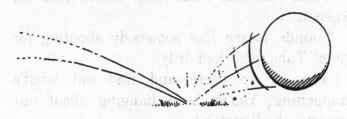

8 Foggy Fools

'We must be mad trying to play a game of football in this!' cried Tubs.

'We *are* mad!' cackled Sanjay. 'We all take after our skipper.'

Tubs peered upfield through the dense fog. 'What's going on, any idea?'

'Nope, not a clue,' said the Swifts' goalie, shaking his head. 'Last time I saw the ball was when it suddenly flew across our penalty area and disappeared again.'

'Perhaps they've already abandoned the match and forgotten to tell us!'

They laughed at such a ridiculous notion, but then looked at each other. 'Nah!' said Sanjay. 'They wouldn't go and do a thing like that — would they?'

'Maybe they don't even realize we're still out here.'

'I can still hear something, listen,' said the keeper.

'Sounds to me like somebody shouting for help!' Tubs remarked drily.

'You go up there and find out what's happening. You've been hanging about our goalmouth all match.'

'That's so I know where I am. If I wander too far away, I might never be able to find my way back again.'

'Don't be such a big coward, go on. You're playing everybody onside.'

'Huh! How can anyone tell? Ref and linesman can't see anybody more than ten metres away from them.'

As Tubs began to venture forward cautiously, he was almost trampled upon by a horde of green shirts as their opponents suddenly charged out of the fog towards the Swifts' goal.

'Sanjay!' Tubs screamed. 'They're here. Watch out!'

Sanjay was too slow to react. Without further warning, something whooshed over his head, smacked against the crossbar and rebounded out of sight once more.

'Guess that must have been the ball,' he muttered. 'Either that or a low-flying bird with a splitting headache!'

'Well left, Sanjay!' came a piping voice out of the swirling shrouds of fog. It was Luke on his way by, scampering after the ball as usual.

'Hold it a minute, Skipper!' cried Sanjay. 'This is stupid. I can't see a thing in this fog.'

'Fog?' Luke queried, looking around as if noticing it for the first time. 'Well, yes, I suppose it is a bit misty.'

'Misty! It's a double pea-souper. Get the ref to call it off, will you, and we can all go home – if we can work out which way to go.'

'Not seen the ref for a while,' Luke admitted. 'I suppose he's around here somewhere. Have you let a goal in yet?'

'Not as far as I know,' the keeper replied sarcastically.

'Good. Must still be nil–nil, then. I know we haven't scored.'

'We never do,' muttered Sanjay, but he was talking to himself. Luke had vanished,

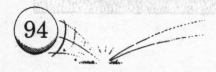

swallowed up by the fog as if in a wizard's black cloak.

'He's a nutcase!' grinned Tubs.

'We know that,' agreed Sanjay. 'And I think he's getting worse.'

The referee was at the time standing near the halfway line talking to the team managers. 'No point in trying to carry on, it's getting thicker by the minute,' he told them. 'Wasn't too bad when we kicked off. At least then I could just about make out both goals from here.'

'Hoped it might lift,' said Luke's dad as Brain

dribbled past them with the ball, heading the wrong way. 'Hey! Turn round, Brain!'

The winger put his foot on the ball and halted, gave a quick grin and then set off back over the halfway line again, Luke yapping at his heels. The men just caught a snatch of the commentary. *'And there goes Brain, the Swifts' fleet-footed winger, but his skipper's not being outpaced. He's up with him in support, screaming for the ball . . .'*

Screaming for the ball and commentating is quite tricky to do at the same time, so Luke switched off his imaginary microphone. 'Pass it inside, Brain,' he yelled. 'I'm unmarked.'

'Keen, isn't he, that lad?' remarked the referee. 'The only way I've been able to locate the ball so far is to pick up his running commentary!'

'Aye, that's m'boy!' grinned Dad. 'He's always where the action is.'

As the referee jogged after the players, preparing to abandon the match, there was a sudden demented cry from somewhere deep in the fog. *'Goooaaalll!'*

The referee had to blow his whistle loudly several times to round up all of the players into the centre-circle and tell them the game was off.

'I don't believe it!' cried Luke. 'I've just gone

and scored a goal to put us in front. We need the points.'

'Sorry, lad. The game will have to be played again sometime.'

'Shame, Skip!' Dazza consoled him. 'Did you actually score?'

'Don't sound so shocked. Course I did!' said Luke. 'Long-range beauty, it was, as well. Goalie never even saw it.'

'I bet he didn't!' scoffed Sanjay. 'I know the feeling.'

'Won't your goal count now?' Brain asked.

Luke shook his head sadly. 'Not when a game gets abandoned.'

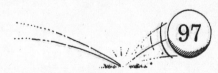

'I've got a funny feeling this goal will,' Sanjay hissed to Tubs out of the corner of his mouth. 'At least in his little black notebook!'

When everybody else had left the changing cabin, Luke and Brain sat together in the corner. 'I'll lock up, Dad,' Luke said. 'I'm just helping Brain get something sorted out, OK?'

'Fine, but if you're not back home for lunch, we'll send out a search party,' Dad joked.

Brain stared at a blank piece of paper on his lap. 'Frosty wants this report given in to him tomorrow. Guess I'll have to come up with some sort of excuse why I've not been able to do it.'

'That's no good. He'll only make you stay in and write it instead.'

'Can't. I'm already doing extra maths at lunch for Jenkins.'

'Frosty won't let you get out of it. He'll stand over you while you do it, if necessary.'

'He'll get very tired legs, then. He could stand there all week and it wouldn't make any difference. Even if he told me what to put, I couldn't spell it.'

'That wouldn't matter. With your untidy writing, Frosty wouldn't be able to read the words anyway!'

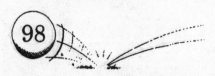

98

The boys grinned at each other. 'What am I gonna do, Skipper? I'm real stuck.'

'Leave it to me,' said Luke confidently, taking the paper out of Brain's unresisting hands. 'I know the kind of thing he's after. Frosty just wants to show Matthew and Adam that the school team doesn't need them any more.'

'But won't he realize I haven't done it? I mean, my writing's huge and all over the place. Yours is small and dead neat.'

'No problem. I'll do it on the word processor and print your name on the bottom. Dead easy to fool Frosty. He'll never know the difference!'

Brain wasn't so sure, but he had no choice. 'Guess so. At least he'll have his report and that's the main thing. Get him off my back.'

What Brain didn't know, never having read the *Chronicle*, was that everybody could spot one of Luke's football reports a mile off, even in thick fog!

Brain nipped into Frosty's empty classroom before morning registration and slapped the match report down onto the teacher's desk. He turned to make his intended quick exit but found his escape route barred.

'Not so fast, young man. Let's have a read of your effort first.'

Frosty slumped into his chair, beckoning Brain to stand by his desk as he tore open the envelope and took out the printed report. He read aloud the headline over the 2–2 scoreline: 'NEW STAR SHINES IN CUP DRAW – yes, not bad, Brian, but better perhaps to be a little bit more modest, eh?'

Brain shuffled his feet, dreading what other embarrassments might lie in wait. Luke had just slipped the sealed envelope to him at the school gate without letting on what he'd written inside.

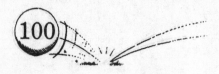

Frosty read on. '*Swillsby's new-look Year 8 soccer team are on the cup trail. They earned themselves a home replay against Millbank Comprehensive when debutant Brian "Brain" Draper, top scorer for the Swifts, lashed home a late equalizer from a clever free-kick routine much practised by his Sunday League side . . .*'

Frosty paused to peer quizzically up at Brain. 'Did you write all this stuff yourself, Brian?'

Brain managed a little shrug. 'Well, I had a bit of help,' he confessed reluctantly, hoping that such a vague answer might suffice.

'Hmm, only giving the Swifts all this glowing

publicity wasn't perhaps quite what I had in mind for the school mag,' mused Frosty before resuming his reading. *'The powerful Millbank outfit scored early on in both halves, but keeper Sanjay Mistry pulled off a series of good saves to prevent them increasing their lead. Then it was time for new captain Jon Crawford to take centre stage. He rocked Millbank before half-time with a superb solo goal that even the great Johan Cruyff would have been proud of.'*

Brain squirmed as Frosty stared at him again. 'Ye-es, quite a lively style,' Frosty drawled in his best sarcastic tone. 'And this reference to Mr Cruyff has a certain ring to it as well . . .'

When the reddening Brain made no reply, Frosty sighed and then winced as he glanced back at the sheet and saw what was coming. *'Although the draw was a well-deserved result,'* he quoted, *'the school might even have grabbed a spectacular victory if any of the substitutes had been given the chance to play a dramatic cameo role in the closing stages.'*

Frosty stroked his chin. 'Well, quite a masterpiece, this report, Brian. You've even managed to criticize the tactics too.'

'It wasn't meant like that, sir, it was just . . .'

Frosty interrupted him. 'Surprised you failed

to mention at least one of these subs by name! What exactly is a cameo role, then?'

Brain stalled for time, struggling to come up with something that sounded similar. 'Well, er, it's a bit difficult to explain, sir . . .'

'Try, Brian, try!'

'Um, yes, it's to do with cameras, like, and . . .'

'Come on, Brian, give me some credit, please! It's got nothing to do with cameras. It's obvious you didn't write this report – but we both know who did, don't we?'

Brain gave up and nodded. 'Yes, sir.'

'That Luke Crawford's on another planet. Why did you let *him* – of all people – get his hands on it, eh? Tell me.'

Brain didn't answer, looking down at the floor, unwilling to admit to his difficulties with writing.

Frosty lost patience with the boy. 'Right, I'll give the honour to the captain now. You can come into this room at lunch and write five hundred lines: *I must never let Luke Crawford play a cameo role!*'

Brain reeled with the shock of the punishment and attempted to gabble out some words. 'Um, er, I can't . . . can't do that . . . sir . . .'

'What do you mean, you can't? You *will*! I've just told you to, lad!'

'B . . . but I've got to stay in at lunch for Mr Jenkins, sir – remember?'

Frosty suddenly pounded his desk with annoyance and jumped out of his seat, making the boy start backwards. Brain thought for a moment that he was going to be attacked.

'Right, you can also stay in at break for me,' Frosty stormed. 'Every breaktime for as long as it takes you to do those lines – if you ever want to play football for this school again!'

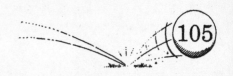

"What do you mean, you can't? You will I've just told you to, lad!"

"B . . . , but I've got to stay in at lunch for Mr. Jenkins, sir – remember?"

Frosty suddenly pounded his desk with annoyance and jumped out of his seat, making the boy start backwards. Brain thought for a moment that he was going to be attacked.

"Right, you can also stay in at break for me," Frosty stormed. "Every breaktime for as long as it takes you to do those lines – if you ever want to play football for this school again."

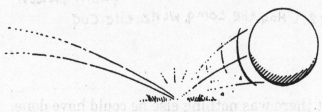

9 Cameo Role

Brain sat hunched over a table at break, facing an impossible task. He couldn't even remember the sentence he was supposed to be writing.

'Ought to make Luke do these lines for me as well,' he groaned and flung his pen at the wall in frustration. It didn't help. All it achieved was to break the pen.

Sighing, he borrowed a pencil from Frosty's desk and scribbled a short note of apology for the teacher.

This time he deliberately misspelt his name, placed the note on the desk and left the room. He

deeR miZZteR wiNteR
i am ZoRRe i kaNot do my liNz i am Nott
veRi gud at ZqeliNg aNd ritiNg az yu kaN
Zee ZoRRe adowte tHe ReqoRte az well
                        fRom BRaiN
9.2. i Hoq tHe comq wiNz tHe cuq

felt there was nothing else he could have done.

After lunch, working in the maths room on the exercises Mr Jenkins had set him, Brain was interrupted by the arrival of Frosty. Brain had been dreading this moment, but the sports teacher was no longer angry and pulled up a chair to sit next to him.

'Why on earth didn't you tell me you're dyslexic?' Frosty began.

Brain was taken by surprise. 'How do you know that, sir?'

'I can tell from your writing now that I've seen it for the first time. And I've just had a word with your English teacher.'

'Miss Elliot doesn't know for sure. She just thinks I am.'

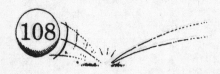

'I *know* you are,' stressed Frosty. 'Because I am too!'

Frosty's sudden revelation was too much to take in straightaway. 'I . . . er . . . didn't know that a teacher might be dyslexic,' Brain said lamely.

'Why not? All sorts of people are. It doesn't stop them doing their jobs properly, even if it means they might have to work harder to succeed. You don't have to let the problem hold you back.' Frosty paused and then smiled before he continued. 'I suppose that's why I can get so ratty when I see somebody else being lazy and wasting their own natural talents.'

'Sorry, sir. I didn't think you'd understand, so I hoped I might get away with it if Luke helped me out.'

Frosty nodded sympathetically. 'No doubt Luke thought he was doing the right thing, but he always tends to get too carried away. Haven't you had your dyslexia confirmed officially?'

Brain shook his head and Frosty stood up. 'Right, I'll make it my business to see that you take some tests soon that will show up exactly what your specific difficulties are.'

'What will happen after that?'

'Plenty, if I have anything to do with it, Brian.

You need the kind of specialist individual teaching that I was never lucky enough to have when I was a kid. People didn't know much about dyslexia then – but they do now.'

'Thank you, sir, I didn't expect . . .'

'That's all right – and don't worry, I'll have a little word with Mr Jenkins and make sure *he* understands the situation too.'

'What about the lines, sir?'

'Forget all about those stupid things! You just concentrate on helping us to win that replay. I've fixed it up for next Saturday morning, and I want to see you flying down that wing. Right?'

'Right, sir,' Brain grinned. 'I'll be there.'

So was Luke, but again only as one of the substitutes, wearing his striped number thirteen shirt. The team was unchanged from the first match with several Swifts enjoying the bonus of another appearance for the Comp.

'Nice to be able to see the other end of the pitch after that farce last Sunday,' said Tubs.

'Yeah, and I hope the ball's up that end more than it is this,' put in Big Ben. 'Gonna be a tough game again.'

'Sure is,' Sanjay said with relish. 'So don't let's

give Millbank a quick goal start like before. Concentrate right from the kick-off.'

This time it was Millbank who were caught napping, their defence cut to ribbons by Gregg and Jon's interpassing. The goalkeeper looked to have Gregg's shot covered until a defender blocked it and the ball rolled into Brain's path as he followed up. The winger had the simplest tap-in goal, with the keeper left wrong-footed by the opposite post.

'*What a start!*' shrieked the commentator, almost taken unawares himself by the speed of the goal. Luke had been busy retying a broken bootlace, but now made up for lost time with a tangled string of clichés: '*One–nil! Swillsby have turned the tables on Millbank, throwing the shell-shocked visitors into the deep end and giving them a mountain to climb . . .*'

The goal gave Brain a surge of confidence and he proceeded to torture his marker, beating him easily on either side. It was looking like one of Brain's good days, and he continued to torment the opposition even after their teacher instructed a second boy to cover him as well.

Sanjay was enjoying a good day too. This was largely because he had so little to do before the interval that not even he could let a goal in. He

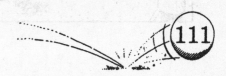

did try, fluffing his attempt to catch a cross, but he was saved by Big Ben's size nine boot belting the ball out of danger.

Swillsby went into half-time two goals ahead, both scored by Brain. For his second, he didn't even need to beat the two defenders. As they hesitated, not wanting to dive in with their tackles too early, Brain sensed that the keeper had strayed off his line and executed a perfect lob.

'Two–nil! An unstoppable effort from Brain into the top corner,' Luke babbled on. *'At this rate, Millbank's teacher will be dishing out lines to his players during the interval – "We must not give the number eleven any more shooting chances!" With the match so one-sided, this is a golden opportunity for Frosty to unleash his deadly subs to sink the enemy good and proper!'*

Frosty, however, was still taking no risks, especially with Luke, although Tubs did give way reluctantly to one of the other substitutes. Nearby, there was another pair of boys equally disappointed.

'Looks like the Comp's gonna win,' muttered Adam. 'We might as well clear off if we can't jeer at them losing.'

'Yeah, Millbank aren't much cop,' agreed

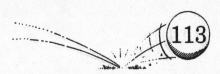

Matthew. 'We'd have thrashed 'em at their place if we'd still been playing.'

'Brain's running riot. Frosty's been dead lucky, Brain turning up like this after we'd packed it in.'

'Huh! Brain-less, you mean,' Matthew snorted. 'Let's heckle him a bit and put him off.'

'Thick-o! Thick-o!' they chanted, loud enough for Brain to hear, but making sure Frosty was out of range.

Brain kept looking round at them, finding it hard to ignore their continued taunts. He was also astonished to hear another voice, so familiar

yet out of context, suddenly cutting in to silence them.

'That's enough, you two! Either shut up or go home.'

It was Jenkins! Brain could scarcely believe it – and neither could his critics. Jenkins was the last person they expected to see on the touchline. He had never even been known to show any interest in football.

'C'mon, it's getting too crowded round here,' said Matthew churlishly. 'Let's go back to my place and watch the box.'

'Thanks, sir,' said Brain when he next trotted past the teacher. 'They were getting on my nerves.'

'Can't have our new star distracted, can we, Brian?' Mr Jenkins grinned. 'I've come here specially this morning to see you play.'

It was at that moment, however, when Millbank finally managed to strike back. Sanjay misjudged the pace of a shot, dived down too late and let the ball slither through his hands into the net.

Fortunately for Swillsby, Brain killed any possible fightback stone dead. Straight from the restart, Jon curled the ball out to him on the wing and Brain set off on a run, hugging

the touchline. He skipped past one challenge, but the second defender stepped in to do his job and knock the ball out of play.

No-one could accuse Luke's commentary of not being on the ball. '*Brain wins a throw-in and a skilful spectator – yours truly – traps the ball and flicks it straight into Gary's arms. Millbank have been caught off guard, not marking up, and Gary's long throw has put Brain in the clear. He's only got the keeper to beat. It's a narrow angle, but he shoots – and scores! Goooaaalll! Made by Luke Crawford's quick reflexes . . .*'

'Wonderful goal, Brian!' cheered Mr Jenkins. 'I'm glad to see you know all about acute angles now!'

'Brain's a hat-trick hero!' Tubs told the teacher in delight. 'He's got all our three goals.'

Their hopes raised and dashed within a minute, Millbank took it badly, arguing among themselves and looking a beaten side. Frosty checked his watch and decided he'd give Luke the final five minutes as a reward for his help at the throw-in.

'I'll let him have that cameo role he craves so much,' Frosty chuckled to himself. 'He can't do too much damage in that time.'

Famous last words. Frosty was regretting

116

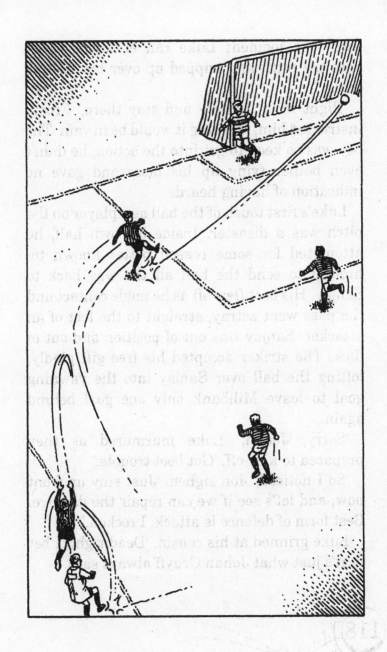

them the moment Luke ran enthusiastically onto the pitch and tripped up over his trailing laces.

'Right wing, Luke – and stay there,' Frosty instructed him, knowing it would be in vain. The boy was so keen to get into the action, he didn't even bother tying up his laces and gave no indication of having heard.

Luke's first touch of the ball as a player on the pitch was a disaster. Inside his own half, he attempted for some reason better known to · himself to send the ball all the way back to Sanjay. His boot flew off as he made contact and the pass went astray, straight to the feet of an attacker. Sanjay was out of position and out of luck. The striker accepted his free gift gladly, lofting the ball over Sanjay into the yawning goal to leave Millbank only one goal behind again.

'Sorry, Johan,' Luke murmured as they prepared to kick off. 'Got boot trouble.'

'So I noticed,' Jon sighed. 'Just stay up front now, and let's see if we can repair the damage. Best form of defence is attack, I reckon.'

Luke grinned at his cousin. 'Dead right. I bet that's just what Johan Cruyff always says.'

Swillsby had another scare first, though, when a long, snaking cross-shot was turned round the post by Sanjay at full stretch.

'Corner, ref!' claimed Millbank loudly when Frosty gave a goal-kick.

Sanjay was a bit annoyed as well that Frosty didn't realize he had touched it. 'Typical! Best save of the game too. Would have gone in if I hadn't got my fingertips to it.'

The Millbank players were still chuntering as Brain collected the goal-kick and passed the ball inside to the captain. Frosty glanced at his watch again, horrified to see there was still another minute left. 'No chance of any injury time being added on, not with that maniac Luke on the loose,' he grimaced. 'This match is ending dead on time, if not before!'

Jon slipped the ball to Luke, but his cousin was too busy examining his laces which had come undone yet again. Even the commentary's sound was muted. 'Luke! Man on!' cried Jon.

By instinct, Luke stabbed out a foot and deflected the ball out to Gregg just before a defender could whack it away and put Swillsby under pressure again. While Gregg trundled the ball towards the corner flag to try and use up a

bit of time, Luke limped into the Millbank penalty area, carrying his right boot. He turned the volume back up.

'Luke Crawford battles on to the end, playing in stockinged feet as he waits hopefully for a cross from the right wing. Oh, Gregg's gone and lost control of the ball. Time to get the boot back on, just in case . . . .'

Luke took his eye off the game once more to bend down, unaware that Jon had won back possession. The captain's shot was half blocked and the goalkeeper desperately lashed out with his foot to try and clear the ball before Jon could pounce on the rebound.

'Oww!'

The football struck Luke smack on the backside and ricocheted past the helpless goalie to bobble over the line. Luke was laid flat out, face down in the dirt, until Jon hoisted him to his feet.

'What a *cheeky* goal!' laughed his cousin.

Luke rubbed his sore bottom ruefully. 'Doesn't matter which bit you score with,' he grinned. 'They all count just the same!'

'Some more than others,' Jon told him. 'That one's made sure we're in the next round of the cup.'

Luke sat in a happy daze in the changing room. He was looking forward to recording their 4–2 victory in his notebook and entering his own name for the first time in the list of goal scorers for the school team.

Gradually he sensed that all was not well with Brain next to him. 'C'mon, you should be over the moon, not looking as sick as a parrot,' he said as a joke. 'Frosty's going to get you extra help for your dyslexia and you've just paid him back with a hat-trick. What's up?'

'Oh, nothing really. Just Matt bugging me a bit. You don't think I'm thick, do you, Luke?'

'Course not,' replied Luke. 'Just daft, that's all.'

'Daft?'

'Yeah, football daft, like me!' Luke grinned. 'We all are!'

THE END

ABOUT THE AUTHOR

ROB CHILDS was born and grew up in Derby. His childhood ambition was to become an England cricketer or footballer – preferably both! After university, however, he went into teaching and taught in primary and high schools in Leicestershire, where he now lives. Always interested in school sports, he coached school teams and clubs across a range of sports, and ran area representative teams in football, cricket and athletics.

Recognizing a need for sports fiction for young readers, he decided to have a go at writing such stories himself and now has more than thirty books to his name, including the popular *The Big Match* series, published by Young Corgi Books. *Football Daft* is the third title in the *Soccer Mad* series.

Rob now combines his writing career with work helping dyslexic students (both adults and children) to overcome their literacy difficulties. Married to Joy, also a writer, Rob has a 'lassie' dog called Laddie and is also a keen photographer.

If you enjoyed this book, here are some sample pages from two more terrific soccer titles coming shortly:

FOOTBALL FLUKES

ROB CHILDS

A new title in the SOCCER MAD series.

The Swifts are facing an important cup-tie. And if they can win once, they can win again. For league positions count for nothing in the cup. Every game is a one-off, and a single goal is all it can take to turn a team into giantkillers . . .

0440 863597

FOOTBALL MAGIC!

ELIZABETH DALE

Dave has something to prove on the Football Magic course – and something to hide. His skills do all the talking on the pitch, but what will

everyone think when they learn his secret?
End-to-end action on and off the pitch.

0440 863589

*Look out for both these titles in the shops – just
two among a whole squad of action-packed football tales from the Corgi Yearling list.*

FOOTBALL FLUKES

by Rob Childs

1 Cup Trail

'We're on our way to Wembley! We're on our way to Wembley! La-la-la-la! La-la-la-la!'

The hopeful chant might have carried greater conviction if dozens of travelling supporters were rocking the coach with their delirious optimism. As it was, a few off-key, croaky voices from the back of an old van didn't have quite the same effect. Even if they did belong to the actual players.

'Quit that racket, will you!' the driver ordered. 'I'm trying to concentrate on where I'm going. And it certainly isn't Wembley.'

'Are we nearly there yet, Dad?' Luke chirped up, undeterred.

Mr Crawford sighed. 'You've already asked me that twice in the last ten minutes. I'm still none the wiser. Ray's got the map.'

'Bet he's got no idea how to find this place either,' Sanjay grunted. The goalkeeper rubbed a gap in the steamed-up, rear window and peered out. 'I'm sure we've been past these houses before.'

Luke saw Uncle Ray's crowded estate car pull into the kerb without warning, causing his dad to brake suddenly and jerk his own passengers against their seat-belts. The car behind, the third member of their little football convoy, almost ran into the back of them. All three drivers got out and began a heated argument over the map in the middle of the road, involving much shaking of heads and gesticulating.

Luke consulted his watch anxiously. 'We should be there by now. It's almost kick-off time.'

'The match can't start without us, can it?' said Titch, squeezed inbetween Sanjay and Tubs. It was a squash even for someone as pint-sized as Titch. Tubs's vast backside took up most of the long seat.

The full-back's rumbling laugh now filled the

van too. 'I wouldn't be too sure about that. It's gonna be so one-sided, I don't suppose they'd notice whether we turned up or not.'

'Rubbish!' countered Luke vehemently. 'They'll know they've got a game on their hands once we get stuck into them. The cup's got our name on it this year, I can feel it.'

'At the rate we're going, I'd tell the engraver to make it next year, if I were you,' Sanjay observed dryly.

Luke decided it was time to take action. 'If you want a job doing properly, do it yourself,' he muttered, climbing out of the van to stop a passer-by and ask directions to the local park.

Luke did most things himself as far as his Under-13 Sunday League team were concerned. Not only was he captain of Swillsby Swifts, he was coach, trainer and player-manager too. Picking the side was the only way Luke could guarantee getting a game each week.

The three men returned sheepishly to their vehicles and the convoy trundled on – just fifty metres to the half-concealed park entrance. They were greeted, for want of a better word, by the impatient, short-tempered team manager of Digby Dynamos.

'You lot are so late, I've got every right to claim

a walk-over through to the next round,' he fumed, brandishing the League's handbook at them. 'That's what the rules say in here, y'know.'

Luke's dad attempted to apologize, but the man was in no mood to listen to any excuses. He turned on his heel with a parting sneer. 'Good job for you my lads still want to play. They're out to break the club record today for the number of goals scored in a single match!'

'Right, men. All ready?' Luke demanded once the Swifts had changed.

'Ready, Skipper,' they responded dutifully, out of habit, humouring Luke's favourite rallying cry before they took the field.

'Remember, win this and we're in the last sixteen,' he beamed. 'We're on the cup trail!'

'Up a cul-de-sac, more like,' grunted Big Ben, their gangling centre-back. 'Reckon we've got more chance of winning the Lottery!'

Luke refused to tolerate any pessimism. 'You've got to be in to win. And we still are, thanks to our great victory in the first round.'

'That was a fluke and you know it. Lightning doesn't strike twice.'

'The Skipper might be right for once,' Tubs cut in, making heads turn towards him in disbelief.

They didn't know which notion was more weird. The idea of Luke being right, or Tubs supporting him.

'I mean, we *are* the strongest team in the League,' Tubs continued, struggling to keep a straight face. 'We're bottom of the table, holding everybody else up!'

'That's an old joke,' Luke retorted as Tubs's loud rumbles echoed around the bare changing room. 'League positions count for nothing in the cup. This is a one-off game. C'mon, let's get at 'em!'

The Swifts, still giggling, trotted out in their new all-gold strip with its bright green logo on the front of the shirts: GREAT GAME!

The kit was about the only thing they had won all season so far. Luke had showed off his un-rivalled knowledge of football trivia in a soccer magazine competition to earn the star prize for his team. It was just a shame the Swifts weren't so hot on the pitch.

This morning, they were really caught cold. The Dynamos had been warming up for twenty minutes, increasingly annoyed at being kept waiting. Now they were like dogs suddenly let off the leash, tearing around the field, chasing and snapping at everything that moved. There seemed to be twice as many red shirts on the pitch as gold, and Luke's dad had to convince himself otherwise. He counted them to make sure.

Unbelievably, the Swifts' goal remained intact, adding to the home team's frustrations. Sanjay's superstitious habit before the kick-off of jumping up to touch the crossbar to bring him luck appeared for once to be working. At least, the goalkeeper thought so. Everything he missed clanged against the metal frame or flew wide of the target, as if the ball had forgotten the magic password to gain entrance into the sacred net.

Sanjay's grin broadened as another shot cannoned off his shoulder and looped up over the bar. He gave the striker a little smirk. 'Guess it's not your day, eh, pal?'

'Don't bank on it. We'll have double figures before the end.'

'Should have had them by now,' scowled the Dynamos' captain. 'C'mon, guys. Their luck can't last out much longer. Once we get the first, the floodgates will open.'

The Swifts' skipper of course didn't see it like that at all. But then Luke's rose-tinted view of the game was always different to everyone else's.

As usual, he broadcast it to the world as he charged madly around after the ball, trying in vain to get a kick. It was not so much a running commentary as a stop-start, puff and pant one.

'Another great save by Sanjay Mistry, the Swifts' courageous custodian. He saw the ball late but got his body well behind it to concede the corner. Skipper Luke Crawford now organizes his team's marking at the set-piece, picking up the dangerous number eight himself. The ball swirls over into the goalmouth and . . . Uuuughh!'

The commentary was abruptly cut off as though someone had pulled the plug out of the socket. Luke had been flattened by the number eight's soaring leap for the ball. He felt like he'd been struck by a jumbo jet, but the impact of bodies was just enough to spoil the attacker's aim. The ball shaved a layer of rust off the outside of the upright as it zoomed by.

Not that Luke saw what happened. He was still eating dirt, face down in the six-yard box. He would have appealed for a foul if he'd had any breath left to do so. Or if he could have spat the piece of mud out of his mouth in time.

With the commentator left speechless, it was just as well that the match wasn't being televised live. The only camera on the ground was operated by Uncle Ray, roaming around the touchline. Luke liked to have the Swifts' games videoed in order to study where things had gone wrong. The analysis usually took him a very long time.

'Think I'll edit this bit out,' Luke decided, looking as if he'd just dunked his face into a vat of molten chocolate. It didn't taste like it.

Sanjay's goal was kept so much under siege that the Dynamos' keeper was relieving his boredom by leaning on a post and chatting to a couple of friends. He'd only touched the ball twice. And one of those was a hoofed clearance from a sympathetic back-pass to give him something to do.

The next time he had contact with the ball was to pick it, red-faced, out of the back of his net. Distracted by a joke, he failed to appreciate the danger when the visitors' left-winger set off on a meandering dribble. He wished now he'd left hearing the punchline till later.

Brian Draper, Brain to his teammates, was the one player that the Swifts boasted of true quality. Naturally two-footed, Brain's fancy footwork turned his baffled marker inside-out so many times that the boy's knickers must have gotten into the proverbial twist. Perhaps that was why he finally tripped and fell over, leaving Brain clear to torment somebody else.

The winger's next trick was to perform a perfect nutmeg. He slipped the ball cheekily through another defender's legs, nipped round him to collect it again and then cut inside for goal.

'Watch out!' screamed the captain to wake up his dreamy goalie. 'He's going to shoot.'

Too late. The shot was already on its way. It wasn't hit with any special power, but the ball curled in a graceful arc towards the far corner of the goal. The keeper scrambled desperately across his line, as if chasing a loose piece of paper in the wind, but he was never going to catch it in time. The net did the job for him.

'One–nil!' exulted Luke, making no effort to keep any note of bias out of his commentary. 'A flash of magic from Brain and the Swifts are ahead. Some people might say it was against the run of play, but who cares? This is the cup! Anything can happen!'

FOOTBALL MAGIC!

by Elizabeth Dale

CHAPTER 1

'Quick, Kaz, pass! To me!' screamed Gary. 'Now!'

Karen paused in mid-run. Gary was being marked by someone twice his size, whereas she had a clear run to the goal. She had to go for it. She chipped the ball ahead, kept on running, drew back her right foot and *wham*! As the ball went sailing high into the back of the net, Karen felt as though she could have floated in after it. A goal! She'd scored a goal! Everyone came and patted her on the back; it was the most brilliant moment of her life.

'Fantastic!' cried Dave.

'Nice one, Kazza!' said Spike, ruffling her shoulder-length black hair.

Karen smiled at her mum and Suzie, who were madly jumping up and down on the touch-line. It was the most magical moment. To score a goal for her school team was one thing, but to score a goal in the final of the Inter-Schools Challenge Cup was something else!

As she ran back to the centre spot, Gary came running up to her. She grinned at him.

'Why didn't you pass it to me?' he snarled. 'I can't stand stuck-up girls who hog the ball in the hope that one day they might get round to scoring!'

She stared at him. 'I couldn't . . .' she began. 'I didn't . . .'

'Push off, Gary!' said Dave, who'd heard him. 'You're only jealous because she's better than you.'

'Girls shouldn't be allowed in the team,' said Gary. 'Everyone knows they only ever get the ball because some boys let them.'

The whistle blew and Karen was soon immersed in the game, all thoughts of

Gary gone. There were only twenty minutes left; they were only one goal ahead – they mustn't let their guard slip. It was a hard match, and everyone was tired. Probably most tired of all was Karen's mum, she hadn't stopped yelling since the game started!

'Come on Garrett Street Middle School!' she called, as they went on one final attack. Spike passed the ball to Dave out on the wing; he ran, side-stepped the opposition, pushed it across to Karen – there was just the goalie between her and the open goal.

'Kazza!' cried Gary to her right. This time he was unmarked. She kicked it to him, he turned, aimed the ball at the net, and missed. Everyone groaned.

'Why didn't you shoot?' Spike yelled at her. 'Dave laid it on perfectly for you, you were in front of the goal, you had a brilliant chance and you passed it back out again to Gary. Are you chicken, or something?!'

'No!' said Karen, indignantly. How could she explain that she'd had her moment of glory, she'd wanted to let someone else have a triumph, too? Above all else, she wanted to be accepted as a proper part of the team. But the Forest goalkeeper had already kicked the ball up to the other end of the field, there was no time to argue.

There were another ten hectic, nail-biting minutes, in which it seemed absolutely certain that Forest School would score at least five goals, but somehow they kept missing. And then, at last, the final whistle blew. They'd won the Cup, and all thanks to Karen's goal!

Everyone hugged each other in glee. They were all talking at once, comparing experiences and congratulating each other, including the other team. For Karen, to be part of the team, to win, it was like Christmas and all her birthdays rolled into one. And then, as they all walked up to the table at the end of the pitch to collect the Cup, the most terrible thing happened. Karen could feel tears welling up in her eyes. She mustn't cry, she mustn't! Everyone would think she was a real drip! Quickly she wiped her sleeve across her eyes, and stood in line with the others as Spike, their captain, collected the Cup. Everyone cheered. Everyone, that is, except Karen's mum, whose voice had finally packed up. She was wiping her eyes, as though . . . no! She mustn't! Karen glared at her.

The Cup was passed round everyone, someone produced a camera, a reporter from the local paper wanted to know what Karen's name was, and then they all went in to get changed.

'I'm sorry I fluffed that chance you gave me to score again,' Karen said to Dave as they walked off the pitch.

'Oh that doesn't matter!' he said. 'You scored the first time, and we won, didn't we? That's all that counts!'

'Yes,' said Karen. 'It was a brilliant game!'

'Do you know,' said Suzie, 'when they handed Spike the Cup, I was so proud, I felt like bursting into tears, and I wasn't even in the team!'

Karen smiled at her, gratefully. She couldn't have admitted such a thing to anyone. 'How about coming round to my house afterwards?' she suggested, as Dave joined them. 'My mum's made a special celebration cake – and I could do with some help eating it.'

'How did she know we were going to win?' asked Dave.

'She didn't. If we lost she was going to give me a big piece to take with my lunch every day to make me feel better.'

'She's all right, your mum!' said Dave. 'I'm really glad we won.'

'So am I,' said Karen, pulling a face. 'You haven't tasted her cake, yet!'

The cake was actually one of Karen's mum's better efforts, which was a real shame, because Karen had invited the whole team round, as well as Suzie, to help her eat it up. Everyone came, except Gary.

'Don't worry about him,' said Steve. 'He's just sulking because he was only first reserve.'

'Yeah!' said Spike. 'He was really annoyed when you were picked to be in the team instead of him, Kaz. Do you know, he was even thinking of appealing against the result on the grounds that we had a girl in our team!'

'But you won!' exclaimed Suzie.

'I know,' said Spike. 'Just think what

a fuss he'd have created if we'd lost!'

'Hey, have you heard about Football Magic?' asked Steve.

'Yeah, it's what we were today,' said Spike. 'Absolute magic!'

Everyone laughed.

'I know,' said Steve, 'but it's also the name of a football training course they're running in the Easter holidays.'

'Really?' gasped Dave.

'Where?' demanded Spike.

'In Manchester. And someone from our school is going to get a place. There'll be special coaching and matches and expert training sessions. There's a notice on the board. There are going to be trials for it at school next week.'

'Wow!' exclaimed Karen. 'What I wouldn't give to go on that! How long does it last?'

'A week. But it costs eighty pounds.'

'Is that all?' said Karen. 'That's no problem, is it, Mum?'

Karen's mum opened her mouth to argue, but only a croak came out.

'I wonder who'll be picked to go. Who wants another piece of cake?' asked Karen, happily.